AFRICAN
HEARTSTRINGS

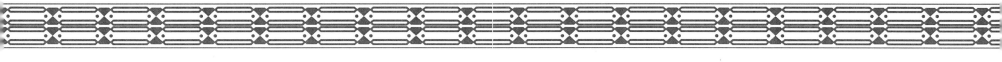

Diane S. Sepler

ISBN 978-1-63630-278-2 (Paperback)
ISBN 978-1-63630-279-9 (Hardcover)
ISBN 978-1-63630-280-5 (Digital)

Covenant Books, Inc.
11661 Hwy 707
Murrells Inlet, SC 29576
www.covenantbooks.com

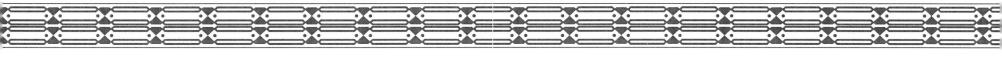

DEDICATION PAGE

Special thanks to Donald and Garrison for providing me with the VISTA and comfort of a most extraordinary venue from which to write.

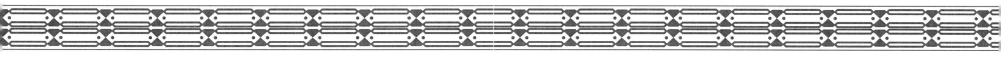

APPRECIATION PAGE

The author wishes to thank and appreciate the following persons who were available and eager with expertise, to please during the process of creating this book. I am forever thankful…

Artist/Illustrator

Ramon Oscar Lopez

Sword & Book Studio

Ramon was born and raised in Miami, FL. He has studied visual art extensively since his youth. Ramon attended the prestigious New World School of the Arts in Miami. He majored in illustration at the Art College of Design in California. He also holds a graduate degree in Art Education from Florida International University. Ramon shares his time between art, family, and teaching. He seeks to represent the natural world in all its splendor and vulnerability. Ramon lives and works in Miami, FL.

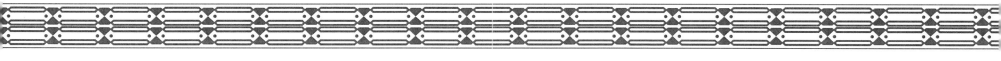

APPRECIATION PAGE

Special appreciation and thanks for their expertise:
  Suzy Carr: Covenant books, Acquisitions agent
  Michelle Holmes: Covenant books, Publication Assistant
  Lilia Garcia: for providing illustrator, Ramon O. Lopez, gracias!
  Diane Deen: friendship, kindness, and assist with illustrator

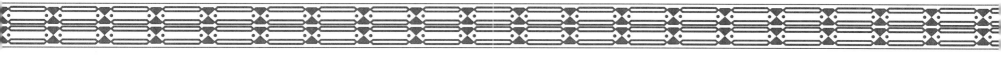

PROLOGUE

Welcome to the wonders of the Animal Kingdom and thank you for selecting my book! As you prepare to read African Heartstrings, I hope you will be moved to participate in the protection of the endangered species and all animals, including us here on our planet. Also, to support in all ways possible to our planet's environment and ensure the many enjoyments of this magnificent world in which we all inhabit for those of us here today, for you and your future offspring, family, friends, and the world in general!

Enjoy the read!

Chapter 3 Flamingo Oasis - Kalahari Desert

CHAPTER 3

CHAPTER 3

Front Cover Wraparound

African HEARTSTRINGS

African HEARTSTRINGS

X

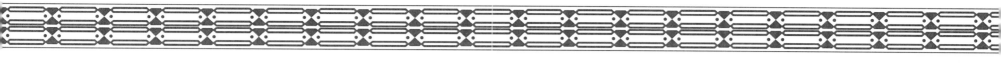

OUR CHARACTERS

Diane Gee—A bright inquisitive young girl, eager to race into life with all of its pleasures. Diane is pretty mature but still a young, fun-loving girl, loving, caring, thoughtful, and definitely not selfish! Diane Gee has been and is being exposed to a fascinating life of experiences by her auntie, some of which she will share with you! Her friend, acquaintances, and followers. But most significant about Diane, she *loves, loves, loves animals*!

Her friend and sidekick, invited on this adventure by Diane's auntie, is Scott, who shares in her intense love of animals! Any wild, furry, feathered, trunked, clawed animal specimen on this *planet*! Scott is very playful, loves reading, soccer, running, and jumping! Scott is rambunctious, boisterous, and almost-always *loud*! A bit of a daydreamer, but always considerate. And he loves Auntie as if she is his own.

Auntie, host of this adventure—A vivacious, exciting, well-traveled, extremely well-organized businesswoman. An intuitive, thorough, wise, generous, animal-loving woman; tender of heart, thought, and deed. No children, Diane Gee is her godchild.

Scott—Diane Gee's neighbor and close friend; a very lucky guy who Auntie has invited for this safari!

EUROPE

Atlantic

A

F

Equator

R

Indian

I

C

Ocean

Ocean

A

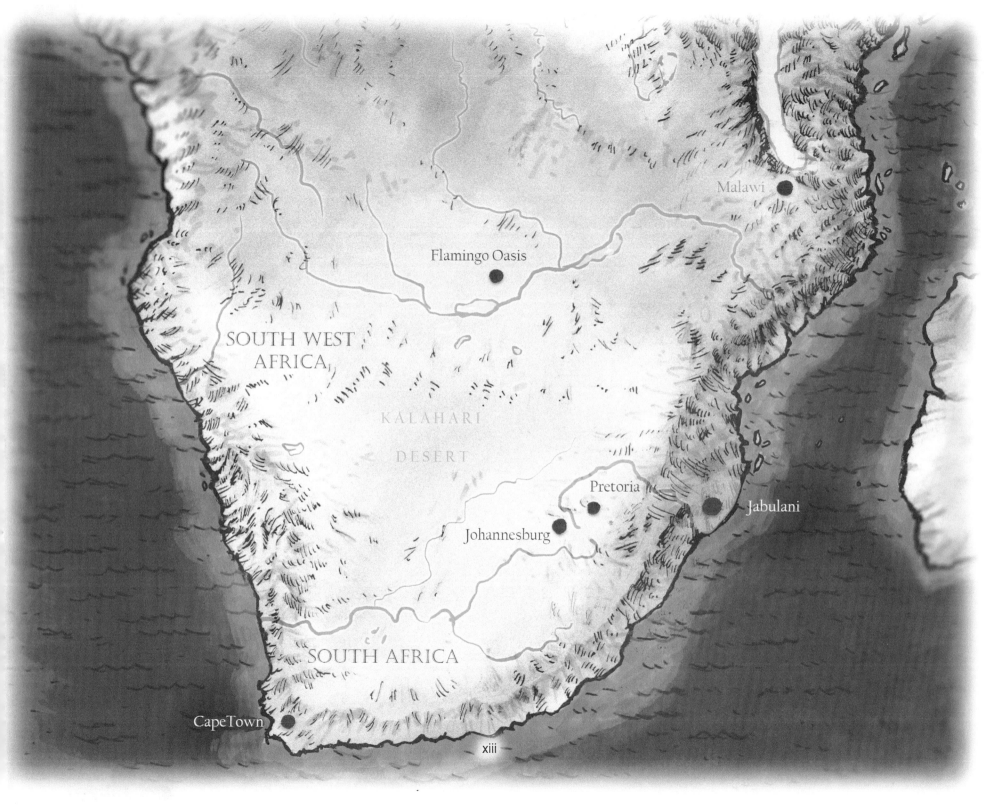

Malawi

Flamingo Oasis

SOUTH WEST
AFRICA

KALAHARI

DESERT

Pretoria

Johannesburg

Jabulani

SOUTH AFRICA

CapeTown

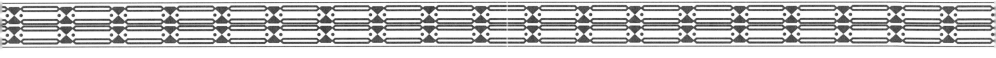

CHAPTER 1

Once upon a time—no!

Once upon a memory!

To memories—A tale!

There was great and specific attention paid by all concerned in preparing for the safari. A month's trip with such a variety of venues requires much consideration, thought, planning and preparation! All made lists and compared with one another to be sure they would not forget any item they would need. It was also decided not to duplicate certain items all could use to save space and weight! They would be flying in some small planes with weight and space limitations, so one needs to think when packing.

- Reading and downtime material
- Clothing for each activity—New and older things we could leave behind, leaving room for purchases en route. Good time to think of others who could use our castoffs in good condition we could share.
- Footwear—Comfort, utility, and style must be evaluated

- Toiletries
- Travel comforts—Within reason
- Notebook, pen, etc.
- Cameras—Be sensible
- Snacks—*Few*
- Most important to take with us: Patience, understanding, tolerance, kindness, and appreciation and lots of consideration for others.

Auntie has designed and created our adventure. She is an expert traveler, and we listen to each and every word and think how each relates to us and our enjoyment and the enjoyment of the three of us and those around us on this epic journey to Africa.

There is such excitement, anticipation, and some thoughts of separation from *home*!

An enormous bite of life, soon to come.

Hard to sleep this night for Diane Gee and Scott!

And so on, onward, onward—to Africa!

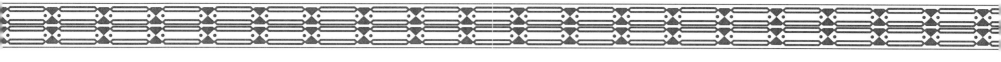

CHAPTER 2

We depart New York City. A day later, we arrive in Johannesburg, the Republic of South Africa.

Scott says, looking out the window of the plane arriving in Johannesburg, "My stomach is jumping—I feel wild. I'm a little scared but so, so grateful to be along for this ride!"

The Johannesburg Hotel property is enormous on a large piece of land, with huge beautiful trees and ponds. The hotel is grand and has very high ceilings with furniture and many pieces of art and lore of the land. We cannot wait to run and stretch our legs after over a day of traveling.

Auntie has arranged for us to be shown around the property, move, run, and enjoy the surroundings. We will meet her for tea in thirty minutes. The trees on the property are ancient and huge and provide shade over a big area. Scott wants to climb one!

"He is such a boy," exclaims Diane Gee to the gentleman accompanying them.

Scott and I run and race about, with lots of pent-up energy.

Scott kicks up his heels and runs and shouts with glee!

Thirty minutes passes quickly. We return to the hotel and wash our hands in a beautiful powder room.

We are taken to the tea room to meet Auntie for tea, sandwiches, and, sweet cakes, overlooking a lake with flamingos parading by!

Note: Diane's favorite color is *pink*!

Scott exclaims, "Wow!" as he digs into a small tea sandwich—he has *three*!

We can't wait to bathe for dinner. The hotel bathrooms are huge. We each have a bathroom; each has a big picture window overlooking the gardens and ponds—and flamingos; Diane Gee is in heaven; after all, they are *pink*!

Scott's window looks into the branches of a giant tree where he observes a bird's nest! He goes crazy, and we all must go to look. It is adorable, as is Scott.

We bathe. Before Scott dresses, he comes bounding out into the living room—in an *oversize robe*. Scott's robe is too big for him. He is too adorable. Auntie and Diane Gee give him a big hug!

We dress and leave for dinner. Our guide for Johannesburg meets us at dinner and advises of the plan for our next day. Auntie has planned the following:

- Tour the city
- Learn of the local activities, businesses in Johannesburg
- And a diamond mine visit

We leave early next day to tour the city. Johannesburg is a very diverse city with people from the entire African continent, India, Europe, etc. It is a very large, crowded, but interesting city.

The diamond mine visitation is very active, dirty, crawling with people picking through the hole, many people, some machines, incredible worker activity but interestingly action moves slowly!

We are taken to a small studio and shown diamonds of various sizes and brilliance.

Scott says, "Not like Cartier nor Graff."

Diane Gee says, *"Scott!"*

But Scott's mom is a shopper, and he goes with her on occasion, so he has some knowledge.

As we return to the hotel for lunch, Auntie and Scott discusses the 4Cs.

Diamond 4Cs:

- Carat
- Color
- Clarity
- Cut

Diane Gee says, "I'm learning also. It's important as one day, I'll be selecting a diamond. I want to be knowledgeable and select a *good one*!"

Auntie smiles. "Smart girl."

During lunch, we are told of uprisings in the barrios, causing concerns in the region. As a result, the hotel has prepared the following activities for the guests—in-house.

An afternoon lecture about Nelson Mandela and his effect on the continent and an African bazaar of arts and crafts, of the region and the continent, and an evening featuring a celebratory dinner with local personalities, music, and dancers.

We love the arts and crafts bazaar! Scott hops around to the tribal music, and we all enjoy the local arts and crafts. However, the children are bothered and greatly concerned about the animal-skin rugs and parts of animals used as tables and stools.

Scott cries, "How could they!"

A discussion is begun, which continues through the journey, about animal cruelty, vegetarianism, leather shoes. It is a very complicated disturbing conversation—not to be solved today. We walk back to our rooms, arms about each other, almost in silence. Life, it seems, is sometimes very cruel.

We get into bed and talk and talk until sleep overcomes us! We are ready to leave in the morning for Pretoria.

Glossary

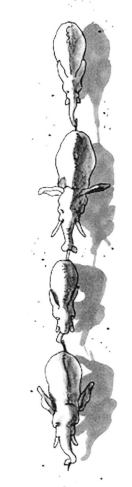

Chapter 2:

Lore ~ history
Diverse ~ unlike
Carat ~ gem size
Barrios ~ slums
Celebratory ~ party

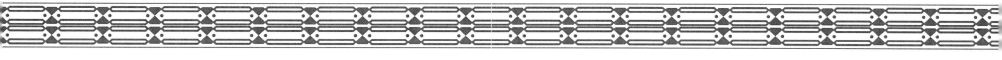

CHAPTER 3

All out of the hotel, all into the helicopter. Helicopters are new to the children. Scott is in the front with the pilot, jibber jabber. He thinks he may like to be a copter pilot. Auntie thinks, *I wonder how his mother will relate to that idea*!

It is a short hop to the small township of Pretoria. All are thrilled to have the helicopter experience. Pretoria, birthplace of Nelson Mandela, the father of South African freedom. We are taken to visit his home and learn of his life. We are like sponges and absorb all we can.

Scott and Diane marvel such a man could come from this tiny community. There is much, much more to be learned about Mandela. Auntie purchases a book for us to learn more of the dedicated man and his long somewhat-tortured life. We arrive at the Pretoria Train Station.

THE BLUE TRAIN. The blue train is a vintage Orient Express train from the late eighteenth century, made in Europe. The Orient Express became the prized mode of travel in Europe, from the late 1800s up to now, through the Alps and now well beyond. These vintage trains have and are being refurbished and sold to major travel facilities about the globe.

We are ecstatic as we board the blue train, which will be transporting us to Cape Town, on the Atlantic Coast of Africa. Cape Town—the grand lady of South Africa!

We are immediately aware of this train's past Glory as we are ensconced in the manner of that day! We are taken by the porter to our sleeping car. We all look at one another and *giggle*! It is the entire car! Fine antiques abound, lace curtains, period furniture, and lighting like we have never seen. There is classical music playing, and when we walk into the bathroom—Scott falls to the floor in shrieks of laughter, kicking his feet!

"Auntie, Auntie, we could all fit in the bathtub at the same time." He is so outrageous and boisterous. He is such a *boy*! Adore him!

The porter who brought us wonders if something is wrong and looks in such a quizzical way. Scott and I run and hug him and assure him we love our rooms. We love this train, and we love him as well! He is befuddled, but he helps us settle in with kindness and care.

Once settled, we are eager to tour the train. So he takes us on a stroll through the dining car, which is attached to our sleeping car. The dining car is amazing and so very, very charming. Auntie is so impressed with the interiors and the refinement of the installation. She's so observant, and it rubs off on us. We now cannot wait for dinner, which is *black tie*.

Auntie says we should go to the parlor car to view the departure from the station. We observe much fun—balloons, a band, and school children singing; all the train guests are waving as we depart the station. Scott and Diane receive a bunch of balloons and are giddy with joy.

"Hip, hip hooray!" says Scott.

Scott is dancing about so enthusiastically, such fun. *Really* love this kid! We return to our car to rest, *bathe*, and prepare for dinner. Which, it seems, will be another experience! Bathing—we love bathing on this continent; it is so much *fun*! There is a large window by the tub, and the countryside is passing by in all its interesting splendor.

Auntie draws a delightful bath with salts and bubbles; the room is rich with scent, the sun is pouring through the window—we could all become addicted to this!

When we are dressed—black tie—we meet in our living room. Scott says, "I'm embarrassed to be in this tuxedo."

"No, no, you look so handsome, Scott," says Auntie. "Let's take a few photos…"

"Diane Gee looks very pretty in her favorite colors, shades of pink. The girls both look very pretty and special. And I look pretty good too, everyone says so," says Scott to himself.

On the way to dinner, we detour to visit the library in the caboose. There are many lovely books, a bar for tea, coffee, and cocktails. Everything is so exquisite and luxurious, and best of all, one can go through the rear door with a porter and stand on the train terrace at the end of the caboose! Very unique as we move through the countryside and watch the beauty passing by us with very little awareness of the train. Scott loves it!

The conductor comes to invite us to the dining car and our table that Auntie has arranged for us. Auntie suggests there are many courses, perhaps lots of things we may have never eaten before. "Just try everything. And if you like, eat it. If not, leave it."

The sun is setting in the hills, and all is lush and green; we are all overcome by the enveloping beauty. The dining car is splendid, in perfect Victorian style. Auntie tells us of the Victorian era and the refinement of that time of furnishings and fancy men's and women's fashion. Diane Gee is enthralled. Scott thinks, *For me, not so much.*

Scott gets up from the table—just after we are seated—and comes back, with the waiter and a bottle of champagne. Scott stands to make a toast. "To Auntie, for sharing this wonderful trip and country with us. We love everything, absolutely everything, especially the bathrooms. Thank you, thank you!"

Diane Gee gets up and hugs Scott, and Auntie dabs at her eye! It has been such a special day. The sun is setting as we roll along on the tracks. *Clickety clack, clickety clack.*

Scott comes to Diane to tell her, "I love Auntie, and she's not even my auntie. I've been thinking about that these last days. I don't have anyone else I've known for such a short time whom I love—but I love her!"

Early next morn, we have a very special breakfast in the dining car. Sun is almost up, and there are so many choices. Scott, of course, orders too much, but everything looks so pretty and fine. We are all so looking forward to our next experience—the oasis!

Our guide advises us, as we visit our room prior to our departure, to be sure our shoes are good for hiking to this rare area. Scott skips back to our car.

We are very eager to participate and explore! We get dressed as suggested and meet our guide when the train stops. We disembark for our visit to the Oasis. We leave in an open Jeep—no top—and the day is magnificent!

There are hills all around us, all is so *green*, and ahead we see a lake. It is a bit swampy, but we are properly attired. We walk a short distance and encounter *hundreds* and *hundreds* of *pink, pink flamingos*! Their plumage is very shiny in the sunlight; the striking bright-pink color is almost overwhelming to the eye! The sight is staggeringly beautiful, and I am busy taking lots of photos of the flamingos, Auntie, and ourselves. They invite me to be in some of them. This seems to be a girl thing as both are smiling and giggling—*a lot.*

Our guide takes me aside and tells me the story of this oasis, and he introduces me to Fifi and Fillbert, a male and female flamingo. They allow me to touch them; their feathers are smooth and very fresh-feeling, not wet as they appear. However, they don't like to have you near their faces.

I feel special to have had this opportunity to meet Fifi and Fillbert without the girls. We fellows aren't into pink so much, thinks Scott.

We all catch up, we are all very much taken by the flamingos' one-legged stance! Their gracefulness and the staggering numbers—our guide tells us there are more than *one thousand* of them here in this train plaza oasis.

Scott says, "I will catalog this vision in my mind forever."

Auntie smiles and dabs her eye. We return to the train. We wash our hands and have another oh-so-attractive lunch—more new entrées to sample.

A storyteller is our host in the dining room. He tells us about when the flamingos began arriving, the lore and care of the oasis, and the magnificence we are about to witness in Cape Town.

We go to the library car and feast on the picture books of Africa and it's majesty and abundance of animals. Love, love this train. It is so quaint!

Bath time, we can't wait; it is so unique!

We dress, have a drink in the dining car, and share the day's agenda, the mystery of the flamingos, their radiant-pink colors, and their *one-leggedness*! Scott jumps up and jigs around like a one-legged flamingo—in his tux, no less. Auntie takes his picture. He is such a fun boy, so adorable. Auntie giggles with joy!

"Dinner is another tasting and visual delight," says Diane Gee.

Scott and Diane Gee try everything, but there are a few items Scott doesn't touch. Hmm! In the morning, we will arrive in Cape Town, South Africa. Hard to get to sleep thinking of today and the flamingos. Every day is so different and commanding of our attention and our senses!

Glossary

Vintage ~ of the past
Ensconced ~ to settle in
Outrageous ~ excessive
Boisterous ~ loud
Befuddled ~ confused
Caboose ~ last train car

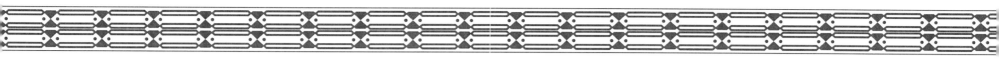

CHAPTER 4

Cape Town is a stunning city with vistas not to be duplicated anywhere in the world. Table Rock, cable cars, rising hills, rocky cliffs, high, high cliffs that drop off dramatically onto the Atlantic Ocean coastline. The children are awestruck at the sight we behold.

We arrive early afternoon and are taken to our hillside hotel, overlooking this magnificent natural and man-made beauty stretched out before us. We organize, relax, bathe, dress, and have dinner on the hotel's sweeping terrace overlooking this city in all its splendor.

In the dining room, the maître d' describes what we are seeing—various landmarks, the port, gondola to Table Rock. Scott is quiet, Diane Gee stutters in amazement. It is beautiful. We are all quiet; it is spellbinding!

Next morning, bright and early, we travel to town where we are treated to a city tour, where we digest the info, facts, and lore of this famous city. We end our tour at an artifacts shop filled with all the wares of South Africa—all types and dimensions.

Scott again is mesmerized by the use of animal parts and skins; he is truly bothered by this. We discuss again over tea in a charming street café. We walk about on our own, window shopping; and when we are collected for dinner, it is spent in an amazing restaurant that cantilevers out over Kalk Bay on the shoreline, where waves crash over the rocks beneath the *glass floor* of the eatery!

Foam is caused by the rush of the water over the rocks beneath the floor, and the water is quite turbulent. Scott sits under the table to be close to the watery scene under our feet. Scott is mesmerized by the power and rush of waves over the rocks; it is scary, we are so close. But Scott loves the experience!

Auntie and Diane Gee enjoy the beautiful room and furnishings while Scott tickles our ankles and hugs our knees! This kid sure makes life fun and interesting! Before we have dinner, we have Scott wash his hands after crawling around on the floor and touching *everything*.

During dinner, we chat about the day. The trip up on the gondola to the Table Rock, the gondola ride proved interesting as the children began talking to some on the folks on the gondola.

Scott observed the universal mix of all colors and types of people, many speaking many different languages: English, German, Dutch, Portuguese, Japanese.

He said, "And we only speak English!"

Diane Gee and Scott both lament that they only speak English, and all these folks not only spoke English but spoke it well!

Auntie explained that in Europe, everyone learns English, their own native tongue, and other languages as well so they can communicate when they travel and conduct their businesses.

When one considers in Europe, many different countries share boarders, but most don't share the same language, making it imperative to study, understand, and speak many languages.

Many questions later, Diane Gee is so interested; and between Auntie and Diane Gee, Diane decides she would definitely like to speak other languages and perhaps become a translator for an international company.

Scott says, "Diane Gee would be really good at that, she is so detailed, curious, and determined. I think that's great for you, Diane."

As we prepare to depart for the hotel, Scott falls to the floor for his last look at the ocean's turbulence, rushing, thrashing beneath our feet while Diane Gee snaps a photo of our boy! We are whisked up into the hills after dinner where we enjoy, from the terrace, another look at this fascinating city.

Tomorrow is a big day!

We all prepare for bed as Scott takes a quick shower after rolling around on the restaurant floor. He for sure could use a great shower! Auntie suddenly calls us to come quickly to the living room by the terrace. Lightning strikes, and the room is filled with light from an approaching thunderstorm occurring over the city and the ocean's coast.

There are three separate storm clouds; huge cumulonimbus clouds aglow with not only vertical lightning displays but lateral lightning, zigzagging across the sky. Thunder, lightning for almost ten minutes, all looks very threatening, so graphic—it's intimidating to say the least.

Scott runs into his room and gets under his bedcovers, laughing and squealing. Auntie and Diane Gee stand with their arms about each other's waist, feeling a little insignificant, witnessing the ferocity, the beauty, and the power of Mother Nature.

After some time, Auntie shows Diane Gee to her bed, covers her, and comforts her, assuring her of her safety and our future.

"Good night, special child. Sleep well."

Auntie dabs her eye!

Next morning, we depart for the southernmost tip of the African continent—the Cape of Good Hope, also referred to as the Perilous Voyage.

This bleak outpost displays the convergence of the violent currents, of the coming together of the Atlantic Ocean and the Indian Ocean. A nearly unmanageable passage in most instances and conditions. It is extremely windy, cold, and inhospitable when we leave the auto to investigate the lookout point.

We return with our guide to our warm and comforting vehicle to digest this significant exhibition of the power of water and wind. And we are told this is a mild day!

It is also an area of the largest collection of big white sharks on this planet! Many scientists and marine biologists come here to tag and study these dangerous creatures and film the efforts of their findings. Some sharks are nearing extinction, which is extremely important as they are such a vital force in the world of water and our valuable oceans! The sharks drastically decreasing in numbers are the subject of many studies seeking to determine the cause of their decline. There is an interesting report to be out soon that we should look for and learn from when published. Extinction threatens many species, all of which are important to the ecology and well-being of the Earth!

We travel back up the coast to enjoy an unbelievably late luxurious lunch at a gorgeous restaurant on the cliffs of the Atlantic Ocean. The restaurant interiors are resplendent in blue, white, and lemon yellow, complete with large arrangements of *lemons* everywhere. Scott goes bonkers over the interiors and lemons!

He makes a major statement to all—he wants to live in a house all blue, white, and lemon yellow. It makes him feel so happy, so comforted, and joyous.

Auntie and Diane Gee are so proud to see him express his interest in design and his opinion. He is certainly growing and refining his taste.

The design is truly elegant, and out here in this almost-hostile harsh environment with the fireplace blazing, it is such a welcoming fortress.

We all have hot chocolate and hot soup. We are so comfortable and relaxed. Interesting that we could feel this way in such a formidable strong physical space, but inside we feel comfy and safe.

We return to our hotel, take a last nighttime look at the glorious city of Cape Town, pack up, lay out our things for tomorrow, snuggle under our duvets as memories are entrenched in our minds.

Tomorrow the adventure we came to Africa to indulge in—the *animals*.

The children are content. All sleep well!

Glossary

Chapter 4:

Awestruck ~ amazed
Maitre d' ~ welcomer
Gondola ~ cable car
Spellbinding ~ breathtaking
Mesmerized ~ taken aback
Cumulonimbus ~ high volume cloud
Veracity ~ fierce
Perilous ~ dangerous
Fortress ~ protection
Entrenched ~ fortified

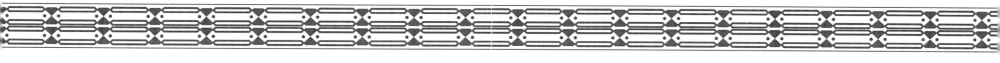

CHAPTER 5

Departing Cape Town, we are flown in a small Cessna airplane to an airstrip in the Jabulani African Wildlife Reserve which is a unique elephant preserve. We are met and taken to one of the most famous and interesting animal enclaves on the continent.

The Jabulani is a compound of low buildings set amid the trees with a moat and drawbridge entry. Birds are singing. It is dry and dusty but most attractive with a strong African ambiance.

We are welcomed by our hosts, offered tea, and in due time, escorted to our bungalow. And guess what? A fabulous bath awaits us in each of our rooms. And we share a courtyard that is lovely with trees and flowers. The girls are very, very happy with this inviting accommodation.

We settle in and move to the grand dining hall to chat up the other five guests. The guests are from France and Norway. Diane Gee chats with them and discusses her interest in languages; they are thrilled to meet her, she is such a smart young girl!

Dinner is exotic of fish and design, and we absorb everything in our minds.

The Jabulani is an elephant preserve like no other in the world.

The next morning, after breakfast, we are about to leave the dining room when, with amazement, we view a pack of pachyderms parading through our lobby! Mothers, youngsters, and babies, one and all—walking through the lobby, trunk to tail, quietly and slowly.

Diane Gee and Scott scoot under a big table displaying a huge arrangement of flowers on top. They are giggling with glee as these enormous creatures amble by the guests, who are mesmerized by their size, gentle nature, and calm demeanor. We all feel *very small*.

The elephants are on their way to a private enclosed garden at the end of the lobby. When the animals have arrived in that garden, the children run to the terrace overlooking this unexpected space. They are not intimidated but for sure are amazed and engrossed in the enormity and gentle manner of these incredible giants.

No one expected this vision and are stunned by their immense size and their proximity to us! It is interesting, the elephants are so comfortable here. We humans are caught off guard and off balance by this unorthodox parade. We are not sure how to react. Everyone is quiet, in deep thought, and we all display reverence.

Soon the matriarch begins to return through the lobby and out the front door and over the moat bridge, with the family behind, *trunk to tail*! Diane Gee and Scott file in behind and are absolutely giddy with the concept of being in an elephant parade!

When the elephants have left the building, everyone speaks at once.

Scott exclaims, "How lucky are we to be in this space at this time?"

Diane Gee says, "Can this really have happened, Auntie?"

There is a tremendous buzz of conversation among the quests. It has been such an unexpected occurrence. All are gobsmacked and overjoyed by the spectacle!

A naturalist is there to speak with us and share information about this unique reserve and its history. The lodge sits on a natural elephant habitat and is a place they know and return to each day! A kind of elephant oasis. They are made to feel very comfortable and welcome here, and they are used to the nearness of humankind.

Watching them, trunk to tail, wander through the complex was remarkable. The children have many questions—some, of course, about their waste, if any. Ahem, all questions are addressed.

We enjoy a visit to the library where Scott entertains, walking like an elephant, swinging its trunk. The guests are very nice to enjoy his antics!

We all share a different kind of lunch, almost tribal in content and presentation. We rest, relax, and look forward to our late afternoon animal trek.

We are requested to dress casually, no heels, hat, and be prepared for an unusual outing.

At four o'clock, we arrive at the lobby and board a Jeep which takes us to an elaborate docking facility. Our afternoon trek is aboard an elephant—one for each and every guest!

There is a wonderful hand-painted platform constructed for us to mount the elephant, and the elephants are in full formal dress! Atop the back of the elephant is a colorful carpet covering, atop of which is a sculpted, painted quite-comfortable chair and umbrella for each of the Jabulani guests to experience!

Each guest is escorted up onto the platform and assisted into the seat on the elephants' back. When all have mounted their beasts, we set off into the park, in single file, over knoll and vale.

The children are enraptured by this opportunity to ride atop such an elegant, magnificent animal. Auntie dabs her eyes as the children board the elephants and head out on the game ride. The children are overjoyed as they travel into the depth of the reserve. Scott is laughing and singing and ducking when necessary to avoid a low-hanging tree limb.

Birds, at times, are following us, and our guide, alongside each elephant, walks with our caravan. Scott is elated; we know we will not hear the end of this for some time!

We arrive at an oasis, and we dismount from the elephants. There, set with a beautiful oriental rug under the trees, is a table adorned with white linen tablecloth flowers, French Bergere chairs for us to relax in, and refreshments.

Auntie has her favorite champagne in a pretty crystal glass, tea sandwiches, cookies, figs, and other local delicacies, served in fine china, linen napkins, and a stunning silver tea service.

Somehow all tastes better when served in such a special decorative way and in such a unique location.

Scott tells the other guests, "Diane Gee and Auntie adore this special attention to detail, but for me, I'll just have a few more tea sandwiches."

As the sun is setting through the trees, we are thrilled to be in this unusual country with such incredible animals. The children are able to feed the elephants in their trunks and touch them, which is a whole experience all by itself. We are then encouraged to board our elephants for the return trip to the lodge. The elephants jog back to the lodge where we all disembark from our perches.

Scott yells out, "Oh my, what a day? How kind and friendly the elephants are…What a wild moment…*Wow, wow*!"

"Bath time is always energetic and loquacious, especially with Scott about. It keeps me and Diane Gee on our toes," sighs Auntie.

After a splendid dinner of veggies, we all retire to the lodge fireplace where there are many candles, a roaring fire, and a few guides and our hosts where all elaborate on their feelings; words rush to everyone's lips, it is quite boisterous.

As all join in in such animated exuberance of this remarkable day and its experiences, Auntie muses, "It must be so rewarding to our hosts to have such appreciative delighted guests."

Next morn, on our early morning game drive, almost as soon as we enter the open reserve, we are directed to observe the imminent attack of a leopard on an unsuspecting gazelle. A most extraordinary sight.

Our guide says, "This is almost never witnessed by man…"

He pulls off the trail. We are very quiet as we witness this ultimate predator hunt for his prey in progress. We see and feel the sharp ignition of the leopard's energy. One can almost feel the coursing of the animal's power through his loins as he downs the gazelle. So flawlessly perfect.

The gazelle only made a small sound and then was quiet as the leopard holds him in place—and it is over! *Over!*

Our guide moves us away so as not to disturb the leopard in his efforts for his sustenance. Such efforts are not always successful, and he may go hungry for days hereafter if the prey gets away.

We were terribly privileged to have witnessed this successful kill and to have shared the vibrations of the leopard's speed, heat, thrust, and immediacy of his efforts. It was absolutely shocking to observe.

It was also alarming to see the herd of gazelles speed away to escape the savage nature of the leopard and his grace in the chase to overcome this beautiful young gazelle.

The brutality, though difficult to witness, was truly sublime when one considers the skill it takes to accomplish same.

Our guide is dumbstruck at what we have seen and shaken as we all are.

We continue our game drive for another hour. We enjoy viewing a stand of zebra and a trio of elephants and a bevy of four giraffes!

It is hard to imagine such tranquility when just a short time ago, we were exposed to violence and death! The children are somewhat numb and disturbed by the aggression, the eruption of force, and the explosion of violence; yet the splendor displayed in this animal encounter for survival, which we had never dreamed of experiencing, is a common occurrence in the animal kingdom!

As we begin to return to the hotel, we are jolted back to reality when our guide cautions us to quickly look into one of the approaching tree clusters. There in the tree branches is the gorgeous leopard with the gazelle he has draped over the tree branches, legs dangling down. The leopard almost has a smile on his face; he seems to be saying, "I have done well and with such finesse and skill."

The children are shocked, and I urge the guide to move on for the children; enough for one day! Silence befalls the Jeep. Our guide attempts to discuss the laws of the jungle.

Scott cries out, "It is so cruel, I love both animals. It is so cruel."

We return to our cottage and have a peaceful bath experience, one and all. We have a rather quiet uneasy dinner conversation, Scott asking many questions of animals manners.

I had invited our host to join us for dinner. He was a major factor in enabling the children to understand a predators' nature and the reality of the wild kingdom.

Next morning, we depart for our last South African reserve. The children are still contemplative as we depart, and they thank all for their hospitality and our guide for his discussions with them about the leopard.

But Scott, as he enters our vehicle to drive to the landing strip, asks our guide, "Please try and do what you can to help the leopard change his ways…not his spots but his ways!"

Auntie is flabbergasted and knows not how to respond. We observe the terrain on the way to the landing strip.

Glossary

Chapter 5:

Preserve ~ sanctuary
Amble ~ move slowly
Unorthodox ~ unusual
Matriarch ~ mother figure
Gob smacked ~ amazed
Loquacious ~ talkative
Sustenance ~ food
Flabbergast ~ surprise

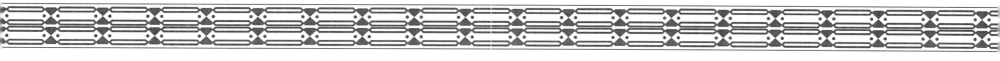

CHAPTER 6

We arrive at the airstrip where a helicopter awaits. We board, Scott sits in front with the pilot. The helicopter elevates much to the delight of the children. Our overview is out over the reserve—trees, water holes, and a bevy of animals grazing.

Scott is especially effervescent as he talks to the pilot with such animation. He is such a delight to observe; his enthusiasm makes us all enjoy any experience even more!

The Malawani Lodge, this is our last South African lodge. It proves to be the most spectacular of all! Here we all share a large residence designed in a very refined English manner, with appropriate service and accoutrement.

Again the bath is exquisite—Jacuzzi tub, huge shower, gold bath fittings, and a beautiful cabinet outfitted with bags of bubble bath, beautiful thick terry robes big fluffy towels, unique soaps, talcum, lotions, potions—everything anyone could ever need in a bath. A most impressive bathroom.

The children run to inspect, and I find them opening, smelling, and trying many of the contents.

Funny how having children along changes the dynamics of any experience. They have so enhanced my trip and acquaintances on this stupendous vacation, thinks Auntie.

Needless to say, we have lots of laundry as we arrive at each reserve, but somehow this stop, we have loads of laundry. We are all grateful and cheer the attendant who collects the nasty dirty things!

Prior to our departure from Jabulani, we sorted our things. We have given gifts along the way and tossed old clothes, so we have some space now in our luggage, and we work our luggage to make an area for clean clothing when returned to be used next stop!

Scott says, "I'm getting really used to packing, and I'm getting very, very good at organization and the importance of being neat. Diane Gee and Auntie have been coaching me about packing during this trip so I don't hold up the troops when we are moving about, hotels, and airports. My mom is going to be so proud of me. I have been a bit of a slob, I think, but the girls have shown me the way which, I guess, I had tried to resist. But when I'm neat, it takes less time to do everything! I'm learning, and I'm happy doing so."

While we are settling in, an attendant raps on our doors, and we are invited into the living room where we see a most incredible sight. Just beyond our terrace which scoops out near a watering hole, there are two elephants having a water fight!

Scott runs to the railing of the terrace, screaming with joy and excitement, "Oh wow! Wow, I love this."

Just as one of the elephants points his trunk at Scott, and he gets drenched. He is laughing and having such a blast. Diane Gee and Auntie are also laughing so hard. The attendant runs for towels to dry our boy! The elephants continue with their playfulness.

We are all having such a joyous moment. So glad to have this child along, he always makes for fun and laughter, thinks Auntie.

Beyond the water hole, there is a family of giraffe munching on the leaves of the trees and a small herd of zebra wandering past, with that three warthogs, scamper past, tails high. All of us are enthralled with warthogs, they are so amusing.

Scott and Diane Gee begin to sing.

> Hakuna Matata, Hakuna Matata.
> No worries!
> What we see is
> A problem free philosophy!

Fun! These children are such *fun*!

We enjoy our home away from home. We rest awhile until our guide, Harry, arrives to introduce himself and advise us what he has in store for us for the next day!

Harry is English. "A fine English specimen," says Auntie.

Harry met his wife, Eve, here in Africa, and he has two children. Eve is a teacher, and she runs an animal conservation school, we see pictures and feel like we've known Harry forever. He is so thrilled to be here at Malawani, the epitome of reserves in South Africa. Harry and Eve's passion is *preservation*—preservation of these lands and of these incredible species on the continent.

And their passion is the animals' right to life and safety from poachers!

We all make time for a luxurious bath, and because we are dining in-house this evening, we wrap up in our big white thick bathrobes, all smelling terribly sweet, powdered, and lotioned—you name it; the kids used everything all over themselves!

Shortly we are called to go into the dining room for dinner. We troupe in, in our bathrobes, all in white, to be treated to a magnificently adorned dining table, resplendent with fresh flowers, an array of lovely china and silver, and an array of unique food, some we don't recognize!

The servers make our dinner an experience we haven't had on this excursion, and enjoying it in our robes makes it that much more fun!

To top it off, we have ice cream for the first time on our trip.

We are all overjoyed to have such a friendly inclusion at our in-home dinner party! Scott and Diane Gee both yell with delight at the sight of a beautiful footed crystal dish of ice cream! Scott jumps up, and we all rise to hug and thank these kind souls who have cared for us so beautifully on this most memorable evening at the Malawani!

After dinner we sit before the fireplace; Diane is writing in her diary, Scott is reading about leopards, but soon, eyes are getting heavy. Auntie escorts the children to bed where, instead of visions of sugar plums in the heads, they begin to dream of elephants, trunks to tails, warthogs, tails in air. And when Auntie is about to climb into her bed, she looks in on the children, and Scott has a smile on his face as he slumbers under his duvet.

Auntie thinks, *I'm sure he is thinking of leopards as he has mentioned leopards oh, oh so many times since our encounter in Jabulani.*

In the Morning

On our morning animal run, Harry, who we already adore, collects us. Our excitement is obvious as we are all talking at once. Harry is driving, and Scott is in the front passenger seat. Diane Gee and Auntie are in the elevated rear seats.

Harry tells of Malawani and its famous guests, like Elton John and his entourage, and he tells us of his vacation he has just returned from and the fact that this drive is his first since his two-week absence.

As we drive into the reserve, we come upon a pride of lions nestled under a clump of big shade trees. Flies are hovering over their faces which are stained with blood from a recent kill. Their stomachs are round, and the king, male lion, has flopped down in the shade with his head thrown back to have a siesta.

Of course, the females have done the work of securing the morning's food, but he is exhausted from the meal.

He and three females and a clutch of cubs are enjoying the breezes on their faces. As they snooze, three cubs are chewing on tails and ears and making the most adorable kitten noises, out of control like kids!

We watch and enjoy the scene. It is so beautiful and lush here. We drive on in our van looking far and wide. We see another of the big five!

A large rhino emerges from a clump of greenery, a big burly adult male; a commanding fellow, dangerous if too close to our vehicle.

He stands strong, at attention. As Harry moves us slowly away, we watch in fascination of this tremendous powerful beast. Unfortunately he and his type are in radical danger of *extinction*.

We are in awe of his hide and of his impressive visible strength. Rhinos are being poached because of the inflated value of their horns. An example of man's destruction of our wildlife for man's own personal desires.

The World Wildlife Fund has a major program in play to save these last few nearly extinct animals, including artificial insemination, zoo swaps, etc., etc., but the commodity of their horns and the demand for its supposed benefits is so strong it has the value of the horn skyrocketing on the black market.

We must support the WWF to assist their important role in saving these magnificent endangered species of which there are many. They must be saved for future generations, appreciation, and enjoyment.

Auntie tells the children that it's important for them to be active in this effort with their friends and family so their children will have the joy they are sharing in the years to come.

Our trail is lined with many bushes, and we see lots of gruffs and a pair of warthogs, tails high, tusks forward, scamper from the bushes as we pass.

We pass through a wooded area, and as we do, we spy a herd of elephants. Harry pulls over and turns off the van. Harry tells us to sit quietly and observe the elephants. As we look about, we see five elephants—three large females and two younger elephants. The matriarch moves in our direction with her eyes glued on Harry, who she has not seen in weeks.

Her trunk raised, she begins to *trumpet*. The two younger elephants follow her and come toward the van. Harry removes his hat to see them better. The matriarch moves to the front of the van, driver's side; trunk raised, she slips her trunk over the windshield and puts her trunk—*on top of Harry's head*!

As she is doing this, one of the younger elephants approaches the rear of the van and comes up to Auntie. Trunk raised, she places her trunk on Auntie's neck and then moves her trunk slowly up her neck, over her jaw, and her trunk comes to rest beside Auntie's ear!

Scott is silent but wonders, *Does Auntie feel or hear her breath*?

This is such a moment. We are all frozen in time.

Harry says hello and touches the matriarch's trunk; she seems very content and happy to feel his touch. Auntie is as a statue as the baby elephant investigates Auntie's being. It seems like forever to Scott, but no one moves.

It seems that when the matriarch saw Harry, her heart fluttered, and she needed to touch him. She seemed to be close to this human being, and when she touched his smooth head, it's almost like she was experiencing a fulfilling moment.

We all are silent and still, tears are rolling down Auntie's face, and Harry is immobile. We are all in a trance mode, mesmerized!

Finally the matriarch touches Harry's head repeatedly as if to say, "Glad to see you," as she turns to depart. As she does so, the younger elephants turn to depart as well.

We are all breathless at this miraculous tender moment we have all shared with this elephant family. As the elephants move away, we are all crying.

Oh my goodness gracious. Oh my goodness.

Everyone, including Harry, is crying and absolutely overwhelmed by this indescribable happening!

Harry starts the van and says, "Shall we return to the lodge?"

We all agree as we are all absorbed by the intense feelings we have all experienced in this last half-hour! We are weeping with emotion as is Harry.

We arrive in silence back at the lodge. We exit the van and enter the lodge where a lovely table is set for us by the fireplace. We all embrace and sob over this remarkable moment we will all forever treasure. The staff is bewildered at our actions.

"What's happened, what happened?"

We learn this is a first for Harry, he has been on this reserve for two decades and has never encountered such a rewarding event with an animal, *ever*!

We are all talking at once, it is bedlam. We find it hard to regain our composure as we hug and hug!

We learn from Auntie, who has been on several safaris, she has never shared such a sensitive meaningful animal exchange.

We continue to share, chatter, and tell all present of this palpable confrontation so extraordinary in its expression.

Scott exclaims he wants to share such with his children, and he's dedicated to devote a part of his life to saving these animals. "I want to do my part to protect these huge, friendly, caring, feeling animals."

He keeps repeating these sentiments again and again. We all sob and keep hugging and touching!

Auntie says, "For me…Nothing could possibly be more moving and meaningful for the four of us than what we enjoyed together this day!"

Next morn, Harry surprises us and appears to see us off. As we depart South Africa, we all long for the day we may return and share with these special wonderful people and these animals who we have had the opportunity to encounter and who have enriched our lives so completely!

As we drive away, Harry tips his hat, and we all are teary-eyed and have swollen hearts.

South Africa, the magnificent!

Glossary

Chapter 6:

Effervescent ~ bubbly
Accoutrement ~ accessory

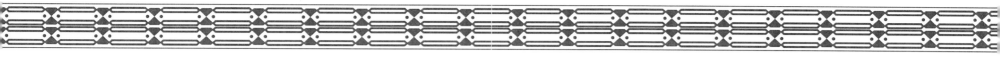

CHAPTER 7

Country of Rwanda on the African equator. Silverback gorilla visitation on one of the volcanic mountains. Rwanda, a country torn by tribal confrontation wherein the Tutsi and the Hutus have been slaughtering each other for years. Two months before our arrival, they had just come to a truce.

We are one of the first tourists to be admitted to visit the gorillas since the stay of the aggression, a kind of civil war, recently terminated.

We touch down in Kigali, Rwanda. The breadbasket of Africa. A lush verdant country on the equator of Africa.

At the airport, we are met by Henri, a giant black man, 6'6" tall with magnificent white teeth and a kind helpful nature. Henri will be our guide during our stay.

As we depart the airport, we pass a parade of tall pretty black women with large baskets balanced on their heads, full of gleaming colorful vegetables, with bare feet walking up the hills along the countryside road.

Scott is taken aback and cannot imagine walking with this weight on your head. "*How*, how, with *no shoes on*!" Scott is so engrossed in this situation. He is so delightful!

On the way to our lodgings we come upon the Kigali market. There is a mass of humanity in this marvelously colorful bazaar of locals doing business. It is Sunday, and therefore, a large crowd is out shopping!

We are a bit intimidated by the huge crowd gathered and the intense activity. Henri suggests we return tomorrow when it will be more comfortable with less people. *Yes!*

We move on to our hotel which will be our home for the next few days. As we drive, Henri tells us of our next day's events. We arrive and check in. Henri bids us farewell until the next day at 10:00 a.m. when we will tour the area and be prepared for our gorilla visitation, update, and orientation.

At the hotel, we are introduced to a lovely lake, waterfall, and a raging fireplace, all visible from a charming lobby. The sun is setting on this tropical landscape; it is getting chilly. We arrive in our sleeping chambers—no more grandiose bathrooms. Everything is Spartan and simple but very, very nice.

We unpack for the last time. We all look at one another—*hugs around*! We proceed to the lobby lounge for dinner and to meet the other limited guests. Other guests are exhausted and will depart early, so they retire to their rooms. We hardly get to meet them. The evening is turning cool, and the fire is so welcoming and cozy. We are happy to be inside as a slow drizzle makes its way through the trees to the lakefront. We are glad to be out of the elements.

Auntie has a French champagne. Interesting to note, Rwanda is a French colony, and all speak French, and many aspects of the French culture is on exhibit here. Interesting, in this basic country of Rwanda, we are exposed to fine French wines, excellent French cuisine, commonly seen French flower staples and arrangements, and French country furniture.

Needless to say, my girls are ecstatic, enveloped in all things French! thinks Scott. We Have a delicious dinner of fine fresh vegetables, delicious lamb, all procured locally from the valley and the surrounding hillsides. We are in heaven; we love veggies.

Auntie has spent months working to secure our visitation permits here to visit the gorillas. Her US Senator secured the permission from the Rwandan Ambassador to the UN, all in conjunction with the Rwandan government gorilla ranger conservancy here in Kigali. We are certified.

Our guide, Henri, has secured our proper papers so we may access the mountains and be able to secure our Sherpas who will escort us up to the gorillas.

The story of this region and the gorillas is best understood by seeing the movie *Gorillas in the Mist*! A film of and by Diane Fosse, a small white woman of intense interest and knowledge who studied these animals for years and finally came here to Rwanda and lived on one of the mountains.

She was often in great danger, often attacked by the gorillas. However, she never gave up, convincing them she was their friend. Soon they accepted her presence among them.

She lived on the mountain and persevered to create this film. The film of monumental importance, in all its glory, has been instrumental as well as National Geographic in saving these endangered giant gorillas who inhabit these volcanic mountains on the Rwandan border with Zaire. The film is a must-see!

On our first full day in Rwanda, Henri comes for us. We are invited to a lecture at the ranger station in Kigali to learn about the wonders of the gorillas and the requirements when visiting the animals.

Diane Fosse's involvement, the region's history, and we learn of the rangers' lives. Sadly during the wars in the region between the Tutsi and the Hutus, many of the rangers were poachers of these great human-like animals. Now they are rangers who enthusiastically protect them and their environment.

Important to know—they now have meaningful employment as rangers of the conservancy, a position of repute, respectability, and security!

We learn of the farming in the area, the working animals, the weather patterns, and the arts and crafts industry in the country. The children are overwhelmed with interest and have many, many questions.

We now move on to inspect the Kigali marketplace. We arrive at the market in Kigali which again raises the problem of the use of animal parts in the region's arts and crafts, and the women's feet with no shoes on the stones and hot surface. Henri describes their feet and the fact that their feet are accustomed to no shoes, and that it is important to know that their feet are tough and almost like the soles of shoes.

We tour the tiny township and return to the hotel to ready for our visit to the mountain early in the morning at five o'clock. We are aglow and happy with what we anticipate ahead.

We arrange for our 6:00 a.m. departure. We have special clothing, we laid out our gloves and shoes for hiking and climbing, backpacks, fanny packs, and anything we may need along the way, bug spray, almonds, small cheeses, etc.

We are anxious and hope we will be safe in the wild world of the gorillas! Auntie assures us we will be safe. We will be with those who will protect us as we wind our way up to the gorillas.

The thirty-seven individuals, the alpha silverback, his harem of females, and their young ones!

Dinner is early as tomorrow is a vigorous, active, athletic day! We are definitely prepared and ready. Scott is so wound up, he kept rolling and tossing, rolling ad tossing he could literally hardly get to sleep this night.

We awake at five o'clock and prepare ourselves for this very active, walk, hike, encounter, and we enjoy a hearty breakfast and check our supplies again.

Henri arrives at 6:00 a.m., and as we motor in at dawn, up the mountain road, to the base of the rain forest and the volcanic mountains, we pass the ladies with no shoes! This morning, accompanying them is a band of goats. We all adore goats!

Along the way, Henri reminds us of what is expected of us in the presence of these mighty giants.

We are fascinated, informed, prepared, for instance, it is imperative to:

- Never look into the eyes of a gorilla (we have dark-lensed glasses).
- Never stand above the chest of a gorilla (we must crawl in on our forearms and knees to view).
- Never reach out or make quick movements when near a gorilla.
- Never touch a gorilla.

Bottom line: be respectful when in the presence of gorillas!

As we draw nearer to our destination, the sun is rising and shining down on the ever-present mist hanging over the volcanic mountains. Finally we see in the distance, a small valley with dirt roads that intersect, thus creating four corners out of nowhere. On each of the four corners is a small outpost, a small one-story building.

On one corner, in addition, there, a group of men are gathered. We quickly learn from Henri, these men are waiting for our arrival.

We are instructed that we are to select from those gathered and that that person will act as our individual Sherpa as we make our way up to the gorillas. They will assist us with our backpacks and aid us in our hike where and as needed.

As we prepare to leave the van, we are reminded of the rules when in the presence of the gorillas, and that Auntie will select our respective Sherpas with Henri.

Auntie and Henri make the selection. We are now ready to make our trek up to the gorillas in the mist!

Diane Gee is thinking during this selection, *How smart is Auntie, and how much I'd like to be like her in every way. She has made all the arrangements for this voyage without a glitch or flaw and with such care and love! How lucky are Scott and I to be in this wild interesting place and about to embark on this most unusual far-from-typical adventure.*

We prepare to proceed up to the mountain and the gorillas. We follow our lead ranger. We pass through an open lowland garden terrain. As we do, I feel a bit of fear, thinking, *Here we are in the deepest darkest Africa, one of the very first people into this region since the war ended…and National Geographic filmed here with Fosse.*

The thought is fleeting, and the full impact of our day takes over my being. In single file, we pass into the garden with the three rangers, who will lead us up till we find the animals. As we and the Sherpas move through the garden, a small band of children run out of a hut at the end of the garden, wearing no clothing and in bare feet, smiling and shouting, "*Bon jour…bon jour!*"

We are delighted to see them. As they come close, Auntie poses them and takes a photo with her self-developing Polaroid camera. She hands each one a copy. As they watch, they shriek with amazement as they visualize their faces developing in full view before their very eyes!

Diane Gee thinks, *Imagine, we take so much for granted.*

Diane looks at Auntie and goes to her side and hugs her with more love than she has felt for another human being! Such an outstanding lady.

Diane is quickly back to reality as we are now at the foot of the mountain. Approached by two more rangers, the one who will lead our entourage is carrying a machete. He will carve out our path through the dense jungle growth in the rain forest. The second ranger carries a large long gun! He is very tall.

The rain forest is now directly ahead. Auntie falls in behind the last ranger with her Sherpa. And then Diane Gee, her Sherpa, and Scott and his Sherpa. Two rangers behind Scott bring up the rear!

We begin our ascent at the base of the mountain into this foreign unknown world! It is nearly dark as we enter as the vegetation is extremely dense and blocking out most light. The ranger, carving our way through the vegetation, makes a path about three feet wide.

It is scary at first, but as we become accustomed to being in such a dark enclosed space, we enjoy the activity, our surroundings, our companions.

We work our way up, up, up to make contact with the gorillas. The tree canopy is almost complete, acts like a roof; as a result, there is very dim light.

We walk and walk up for over *three* hours. We see a few water buffalo near a stream, near the bottom—one of the big five!

We pass a waterfall, and a rock wall looms ahead. The Sherpas assist us by pushing us up from behind and some by pulling us from above.

This is a joint venture—Scott is having fun and enjoying it all, Auntie, not so much! We continue up and are told by the ranger we are on the lookout for:

- Matted down vegetation
- Animal droppings
- And a smell none of which we have yet experienced!

Scott says to me, "Look back, I cannot see from where we came."

The path that just cleared quickly seems to disappear. The heavy mist encourages the vegetation to spring back up after we pass. We walk and walk, continuing up!

Then unexpectedly, the rangers stop. They point out the matted down vegetation along our pathway and the animal droppings—the gorillas are near!

In about fifty yards, we are told to give what we still have—which we are carrying—to our Sherpa. We are all summoned to the lead ranger. He demonstrates the crawl maneuver and reminds us of the demands required of us to visit these creatures:

- Never stand up
- Never look in their eyes (without dark glasses)
- Do not touch
- Should one come near you, curl up
- Don't look at their eyes
- Do not touch
- Stay calm

We get into crawl position behind Auntie and the ranger. The atmosphere thickens. The ranger begins to make a sort of grunting sound as we get closer to the clearing.

The sunlight is now getting very bright. The sound is the sound the gorillas frequently make as they commune with one another. It is comforting to hear, and we become used to and calmed by the sound.

As we come close to and begin to enter the clearing they have made by their presence, it is open and sunny.

Sprawled on top of the matted down vegetation are a large group of female gorillas, their faces black and shiny. Most are partially reclined and eating the leaves on the bushes around them. It seems this is their brunch!

We nestle down to observe these amazing creatures doing their thing! We remain crouched down on all fours, astounded by where we are and what we are sharing!

The rangers continue the grunting sound. Gorillas are on the ground and up in the trees. Babies are suckling on their mothers' teats, lying in front of us, while some agile young gorillas are playing in the brush, climbing the trees and some teenager types are roughhousing among the group, making noise and being offensive to all gathered there.

The sun highlights their features: their skin is smooth and shiny, and their eyes sparkle with a goldish-red glow!

We are also aware of a smell, a strong pungent smell, a smell heretofore unknown to the three of us! The smell of wet fur, vegetation, and a musk smell of the animals—unique!

Scott says, "For sure these guys don't bathe!"

Too much!

All of a sudden, standing up from the bushes is a giant silverback gorilla—all 1,700 pounds of him! The alpha male of this family, of these thirty-seven individuals, he stands erect, glares around at these two disturbing teenage types making a nuisance of themselves.

He stands, pounds on his chest with great bravado, growls, and lunges toward the offenders and strikes one of them who takes off rolling down the hill, over and through the bush.

We are very alert to this activity and the abrupt chain of events. Our ranger makes the grunting sound in earnest. Our hearts are pounding!

We are all quiet! Amazingly almost immediately, a very young tiny gorilla climbs up on a bramble pile, stands on his hind legs, and pounds on his little chest, makes a squeaky growl, and, while pounding his chest, falls over into the matted brush—impersonating the silverback!

We all begin to giggle, even the rangers. But we quickly stop, and the ranger continues his grunting sounds. *Grunt, grunt, grunt.* Order is restored.

We remain in the clearing some time more until it is suggested by the ranger to make our departure. We have visited this family for about an hour.

We carefully, quietly back out of the gorilla encampment to regroup with our Sherpas. At an appropriate distance away, ranger, Sherpas, and we all begin talking at once.

Our guides exclaim, "We have never witnessed such an exchange and interaction among these animals, especially the silverback. And his aggression to the younger gorillas and the baby gorilla impersonating his father…" The guides are as excited and giddy as we are.

To have been so close to these powerful, highly intelligent, endangered animals and to share this unheard-of relationship with them—none can believe what we have just experienced!

We gather our belongings and begin our trek back down the mountain. "Oh, oh, how could this have happened to us," yells Scott in his exhilaration!

He dances around, hugging us all. The smile on his adorable face, we have never seen before such as this! Scott keeps giggling and jumping about, unable to control his emotions.

It is astounding to have had this encounter with these human-like beasts, so like us in so many ways.

As we begin our downward retreat, we again enter the diminished light of the rain forest. We follow single file, and the children begin to sing a silly melody from *The Lion King*.

Hakuna Matata
Hakuna Matata
No worries, no worries
Just a
A problem-free philosophy

Scott and Diane are so exuberant, clapping and singing. Our rangers and Sherpas are so happy to see us happy. The children are so adorable; this scene so memorable!

Auntie brushes tears from her beautiful face.

Memories! Memories! Memories! None shall let this last day's memories on our African vacation be eclipsed from our minds.

We reach the bottom of the volcanic mountain where we have spent the day and emerge back into the full light of day. When we see Henri, all begin chattering wildly. Henri is trying to understand the story and the intense excitement.

We thank our Sherpas and have brought chocolate bars for their enjoyment. We thank and appreciate them again and again, and we all hug!

Our ride back to the hotel is so much fun. Diane and Scott break into song.

Hakuna Matata
Hakuna Matata

A proper ending for this wondrous day in Rwanda!

We arrive at our Kigali Hotel, confirm our exit plans to the airport in the morning with our guide, and make our way to the high tea, underway in our hotel lounge.

Auntie enjoys her usual chilled champagne, we all hug! There are hugs, tears, and shrieks all around as we all thank one another for such a magnificent journey. A journey of love, a journey of learning, a journey of sharing, caring, understanding, respecting, experiencing, welcoming, knowing, and growing—growing out of our very skins!

"We thank Auntie, but with such love and emotion, she has shaped us, our sense of awareness, understanding, and feeling and shown us the importance of other people, this planet, and worldly cultures…restaurants, hotels, services, weather, airport, guides, time zones, etc., etc., etc.," says Diane Gee.

Auntie observes, Diane has grown, during this time together, into a charming, more wonderful, kind, caring, tender, fun, and responsible young woman whose friendship, she witnessed, with Scott was so endearing.

Scott, what fully can possibly explain one's love for him. His joyousness, humor, impulsiveness, love, naivety, curiosity, and genuine manner—one in a zillion!

"This *thing* created among the three of us," says Auntie, "so precious, will never be forgotten, and so cherished, never to be replicated, will be carried in my mind and my thoughts *forever*!"

Glossary

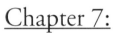

Chapter 7:

Truce ~ stay/cooling off
Breadbasket ~ grocery
Intimidated ~ afraid of
Sherpas ~guides
Preserved ~ continue
Machete ~ large knife

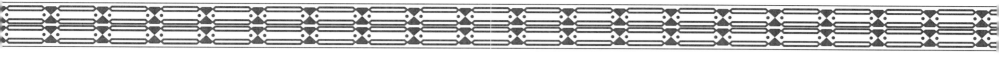

CLOSING THOUGHT

Now that you've shared the magnificence of this planet's animals and have been exposed to the threat to our environment and been exposed to the climate crisis that endangers our entire globe ~ Let's think about how we, you and I, can intercede, make adjustments, and changes as necessary to protect the amazing creatures on this planet and help save a lifestyle! Our lifestyle, with dignity for all on this earth!

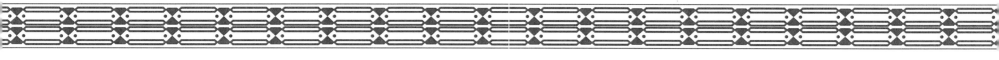

ABOUT THE AUTHOR

Diane, as a first-time author, who, later in life, has sought to write a vehicle to awaken in children the scintillating, inspiring world of animals and travel by focusing on endangered species and the global climate crisis.

The object—to expose the magic of the animal kingdom which literally *jumps* out of this book!

To young people who will feel and be bitten by the passion of love for animals, and will be moved to save and protect animals and their environment for their and their children's future, and to strive to guarantee quality of life for animals as well as humans in this delicate century ahead.

As we travel the globe, travel awakens the soul and opens one's mind! This book releases the vibrations garnered from the beasts, it obviates their innate passions, their focus, and the shocking immediacy of man's contact with them in all of its splendor—so very much more enticing and memorable than the overwhelming contact with the computer! It is so important to have time away from the confines and sedentary practices of the computer and social media! It is suffocating individual thought and the wonders of the mind!

This book was written to provide a child with a timeless rewarding experience and understanding of nature! And to inject into and jump-start children's ability to be sensitive and have real feelings by reading, thinking, and traveling!

Diane's bio specifics: Diane is a perfectionist, achiever, Scorpio, born in Upstate New York in 1939. She was shaped by attending a one-room schoolhouse at the age of three and a half who was moved to third grade in the one year she attended this school, where in one room the first grade was in the first row, the second grade was in the second row, the third grade in the third row.

At four and a half, she was in a regular school in fourth grade in a small city nearby. She was a high school cheerleader, Queen of Smiles, Queen of Local National Guard, attended Oneonta State Teachers College for one year.

She became a Delta Airlines stewardess, based in Atlanta, Georgia (1959). Diane was selected to execute the public relations for the company, appearing on film and in magazine ads and on television to introduce Delta's first jets: the Douglas DC-8s and the amazing plane of the day—the Covair 880, manufactured in San Diego, California, often compared to the French Concord!

Diane was married for thirty years to a very fine person.

Diane was president and treasurer of the Miami Springs Jr. Women's Club (1967). During her presidency, the club was the most successful, financially and award-wise, junior club in the state of Florida.

"Diane was a community activist" (1968–1970) (*Miami Herald Archives* reporter Margaria Fitchner).

Diane was an interior designer (1972–2015). Her work was featured—repeatedly—nationally and internationally in magazines.

Diane executed a major project for Carnival Cruise Lines in the Bahamas in 1988–1990. She was featured in *People Magazine*.

On TV:

- *Rich and Famous*
- *Good Morning America*
- *Entertainment Tonight*
- *Today Show, PM*
- *Magazine, Connie Chung*
- ETC

She won the coveted Gold Key Award, given by the hotel industry for the Grand Bay Hotel in Manhattan for best lobby design.

Diane was a member of the founding members of the Miami Snow Ski Club. She was one of the founders of the Miami New World Symphony established in 1987, established by Ted and Lin Arison and Michael Tilson Thomas, now in its thirty-second year. She was a board member for thirty years of the NWS. She created and chaired many galas.

She established a composer's society, a major fundraising vehicle for the organization. She designed living facilities for the fellows of the NWS.

She was a member of the facilities committee for the NWS center, designed by Frank Gehry, for five years.

Diane was and/or is a donor of:

- Miami City Ballet, board member /honored for her service
- Project Newborn—Jackson Memorial Neonatal Center, created Banyan Club, philanthropic vehicle
- Lion of Juda member
- Founder of Adrien Arsht Performing Arts Center
- Perez Art Museum
- Frost Museum of Science
- MOCA Art Museum
- Founder of Mt. Sinai Hospital
- Vizcaya Museum and Gardens—eleven-year restoration committee chair
- Seraphic Fire
- Wolfsonian Institute
- Institute of Contemporary Art

CPSIA information can be obtained
at www.ICGtesting.com
Printed in the USA
LVRC080028250621
691101LV00002B/32